Punishable by Law

Adriana Blair

DEDICATION

For Father Terry at Saint Mary's Preparatory School who taught me you don't always have to leave room for the Holy Ghost.

ONE

"Brad, please come to my office," a stern female voice crackled over the intercom then he heard a *click*.

Silence.

Brad Thomas, the newest associate at Marks, Smith and Sanders, sighed and rolled his eyes.

"I can't believe I went to Harvard Law for this," he muttered as he reluctantly walked down the hall to Karen's office. Brad had graduated at the top of his class at Harvard and accepted a position as an associate at a small but prestigious law firm in Boston. His tall, muscular physique and deep brown eyes had always cast spells on women, making even the toughest women weak in the knees.

He studied Karen for a moment before knocking on the door. She was turned slightly away, her long legs crossed and angled towards the window where she gazed while talking on the phone, her voice low and confident, dripping like honey tainted with poison.

"No, Bill. They'll never go for that. I'm telling you, think of something else. Fast." She spoke slowly as if addressing a small child.

God, she's a bitch. But so hot. He stared unabashedly at her long, tanned legs, watched as she tossed her straight black hair over her shoulder, revealing full breasts under a deep red blouse. Her black and white hound's tooth skirt stopped just short of her knees and she had red fuck-me heels on her delicate feet.

Karen Sanders had just been promoted to partner in the firm at the tender age of twenty-nine. She was not exactly known for her warmth and kindness, but she had won all of her cases so far and was quickly becoming known as the best up and coming attorney in the city.

The Ice Queen, as he referred to her when talking to his friends, had been utterly resistant to his charms. He was careful not to kiss up, but he did wish she would take notice of his job performance and okay, maybe he wanted her to take notice of him, too. But, the flirting aside, she didn't seem impressed with him at all. Last week, he had successfully convinced a client who was about to fire the firm to reconsider. Mr. Jensen had stormed into the office, frustrated with their new paralegal, Amy, and asked for a refund on his retainer. Brad had taken control, leading him into the conference room, brought him a cup of coffee and talked with him at length about his concerns. Within an hour, both men were walking out of the room, laughing and shaking hands. What was Karen's reaction when she heard the news? A raised eyebrow and a half smile. It was frustrating to say the least. Not that he needed her approval; he knew he kicked ass in his new position, but some recognition would be nice. It was as if she were purposely ignoring him. And he was not used to being ignored by women. He had begun to wonder if she were even interested in men.

She turned to Brad and motioned him inside impatiently. He stepped through the door and she pointed to the brown leather chair in front of her desk. He felt himself grow hard as he listened to her throaty voice, giving orders to the poor soul on the other end of the line. Every few seconds, she would glance over, her round icy blue eyes appearing to look right through him. He tried to force the dirty thoughts out of his mind but it was tough. He allowed himself a moment to imagine what he'd like to do if he ever found himself alone with her. *God, I'd love to bend her over the desk, push up that tight skirt...*

His fantasy came to an abrupt halt when he heard his name. "Brad? Earth to Brad?"

He blinked and took a deep breath. *Fuck, I've got to get it under control.* "What did you need, Karen?"

"Out late last night? Your college days are over, Brad. You have a big-boy job now and I need you to be on point when you're at work. Can you handle that?"

He had to bite his tongue as he suppressed a smirk. *I'd love to teach her a lesson. The only reason she gets away with talking to me like that is because I need this job on my resume and I have to put up with her, at least for a year. After that, I can go anywhere.*

"I didn't go out last night, actually. I stayed in and worked on this deposition. I think when you read over it, you'll see that I can absolutely *handle* it."

Her smile was sugary sweet. "Good, then. Email it to me right away."

"You got it."

***

"Why do you put up with it? Just go somewhere else."

"Are you kidding? Do you know how good this will look on my resume?" Brad looked at his friend incredulously.

Nathan looked like a muscle-bound jock, standing at six feet tall with short blonde hair, blue eyes and bulging muscles peeking out from underneath his tight t-shirt. He was actually much smarter than his appearance would suggest. He had been valedictorian in their graduating class at Harvard. The two had met on their first day of law school and hit it off instantly.

Nathan looked around the crowded outdoor bar, signaled for the server to bring them another round. "I know, man. She just sounds like a royal bitch. But, hey, if you can stick it out for the rest of the year..."

"I can. And I'd like to stick something to her."

Nathan laughed, tossing his head back. "No, no, no. Don't even think about it. You wanna get disbarred for sexual harassment?"

"Yeah, yeah, I know. She's just so hot yet so...mean. I should hate her, but I just want to..."

"I get it. You want to conquer her. Behave yourself, caveman. It's not worth it."

Brad leaned back in his chair, ran his hands

through his hair. "Nathan, the voice of reason and of keeping your dick in your pants. What would I do without you?"

"Probably end up jobless?"

"Ahhh..." Brad stretched his arms over his head. "Where are our drinks?"

The next morning, Brad yawned as he poured another cup of coffee. He had gotten to work two hours early this morning to finish preparing for a case. Karen had walked by his office but hadn't even looked in his direction. He leaned against the kitchen counter as he went over his mental to-do list for the day.

"Pour me a cup, would you?" Karen purred.

Brad was startled. When had she walked in?

He gave her his most professional smile as he sat the hot carafe full of coffee on the counter. "Oh, I'd better let you do that. I might spill it." There was no way he was going to pour her a cup of coffee, act like her little helper-boy. He was willing to pay his dues, but degrading himself and becoming more like her assistant and less like her equal would only hurt him. Not only would he never have her respect, but he could forget about having the respect of anyone else in the office.

She was momentarily thrown off balance, as if she had expected him to obey without question. She pursed her lips. "Okay, then. Well, I don't want you to ruin this," she said as she ran her hands along the smooth fabric of her dress. It was crisp white, with a round neck line and black piping along the sides. It looked almost athletic but was clingy enough to be sexy. And those shoes, those damn fuck-me heels.

They were black patent, reflecting the bright fluorescent lights overhead, sitting on top of four-inch stilettos. He wondered what she would look like wearing *only* those heels.

"That would be a shame," he said.

"Indeed. How is the Swanson case coming along?"

"Just fine. It looks like the discovery process was successful."

"Oh really? They are going to settle?"

"Looks like it. They really want to avoid a trial."

"That's too bad," she said as she pushed a stray piece of hair out of her eyes. "I love a good fight."

He gave her a look. "But isn't the goal to settle out of court?"

She cocked her head to the side and sighed. "Of course. But I like a challenge."

Oh, I'll give you a challenge. "I see."

"We'd better get back to work, kid." She topped off her coffee and strode out of the room.

"Kid," he said under his breath, shaking his head.

Five hours later, he felt his stomach growl. He looked down at his watch. His eyes widened when he saw the time: 1:00. *No wonder I feel like I'm going to pass out. I need to eat.* He had been buried under a pile of paperwork since sitting down with his cup of coffee, which was now cold.

He got up, stretched, and pulled his wallet out of his desk drawer, put it in his back pocket. Deciding to go to the sub shop down the street, he started making his way out the door when he heard a voice from the back office.

"Brad?"

He rolled his eyes. Almost made it.

Walking back to Karen's office, he peeked his head in. "Yeah?"

"Are you going out for lunch?" She bent down and reached into her large red leather handbag. He forced himself to look away when he saw that he had a clear view down her dress. Before he could answer, she continued. "Where are you going? I'd like some Italian today. Doesn't that sound good? Grab me a Caesar salad and some breadsticks from Peppino's, would you?" She held out a ten dollar bill.

"I was actually going to—"

"Oh and extra olives, please."

"Karen, I was going to Sam's Subs. I'd be happy to pick you up something there, if you'd like."

She narrowed her eyes, biting her lip. "No, Brad. I wouldn't like."

Noticing Brad's hesitation, she laughed. "Is there a problem? Peppino's is right next to the sub place. Have you ever been there? It's amazing. You should try it."

Standing in line at Peppino's, Brad was silently fuming. He had never been bossed around or controlled before, especially not by a woman. He thought of his ex, Rachel. She had been so sweet for the first six months of their relationship, but then had turned controlling and manipulative. He had broken up with her shortly after discovering her true personality. He was not one to put up with emotional abuse for any length of time. He'd rather be single.

But the Ice Queen hadn't left him with much of a choice, which was her intention anyway. The only thing more ridiculous than giving in to her would be standing in her office, arguing with her over where to get lunch. He had been really hungry with no strength to fight. *Just a few more months, buddy. You can do this.*

Returning to the office, he sat the white Peppino's bag on her desk.

"I thought you got lost!" she said, laughing.

"There was a long line," he said as he quickly walked out of the room. He feared that if he stayed, he would say something he would regret. *The bitch didn't even say thank you.*

The rest of the week flew by, thank God. The firm was slammed, busy with several new clients and Brad landed a new case. He was representing a man going through divorce and his wife was demanding extravagant amounts of alimony and child support, even though they agreed to share custody of their two children. Karen barely spoke to him all week, which was just fine. The less interaction he had with her, the better.

On Friday night, he had a date with a woman he met online. He hated the idea of online dating, but decided to give it a try. He wasn't quite ready for a relationship but he wanted to keep an open mind. Besides, he was a ball of pent up tension from having to deal with Karen for the past few weeks. He really wanted to fuck her; maybe that's what she needed and she would stop being such a pain in the ass. But, since that wasn't going to happen, he'd have to get his rocks off elsewhere. Maybe it would relax him and he could go back to work Monday ready to face anything, including a condescending and manipulative shrew.

Her name was Sheila. Apparently she was a first grade teacher, raised in a small town in Illinois and had moved to the big city after graduating from Northwestern University two years ago. She sounded wholesome. Although Brad knew from experience that more often than not, the women who seemed the most innocent were actually the freakiest in bed. Something about the Midwestern air, the wide open fields, the little white churches every few miles with the dainty steeples on top...It made good girls go bad and he definitely hoped this was the case with Sheila.

"So what brought you to Boston?" *God, I hate small talk.*

"Well, I have some family here. Also I read that it is one of the best cities for young people to start careers." *Seriously? Okay, she's boring. Still, she might be down for some action later, so be patient.*

"It is a great city." *She's giving me nothing to go on. She apparently never learned the art of conversation.*

"Oh and I love the Red Sox! Being from Illinois, basketball is big, but baseball, not so much. I've always loved it. It drove my family crazy. They think it's so boring." She giggled.

"That's cool, I love the Red Sox, too. We should check out a game sometime."

"We could if it were baseball season."

He laughed. "You're a smart-ass, aren't you?"

She shrugged like a little girl, cocking her head to the side as she smiled coyly. "I've heard that once or twice. Sorry."

"No, I like it."

She drained the glass of her third Mojito and leaned closer to him. "I like you," she said as she touched his arm. She batted her lashes as she ran her fingernails up and down his arm. He smirked. *The girl knows what she's doing, I have to hand it to her. And she's giving me the green light, which is exactly what I was hoping for.*

He gave her a ride home and as he was walking her to the door, she invited him inside. They started kissing right away and Brad pushed her onto the couch. He pinned her wrists down and gently bit her neck.

"Ow!" she said.

Brad laughed and did it again. She giggled and said, "Ooh, you're rough. I like it."

"I thought so."

He reached up her shirt and unhooked her bra. She took it off and tossed it to the floor as he touched her full breasts. "Mmm...you're so soft..." He lifted her up to a seated position and pulled her shirt over her head.

As he flicked her nipples with his tongue, his hands reached down and slowly crept up her skirt. *Lace panties. Nice.*

"Rip them off me," she commanded.

"Bossy, aren't we?"

"I want you now, Brad."

"Good because you're going to get it," he said as he yanked her panties down her legs and threw them onto the floor.

She quickly unfastened his belt, unzipped his pants, and began stroking him.

He pushed his pants down and noticed her eyes widen.

"You're so big, Brad."

"You think you can handle it?"

"God, yes. Give it to me."

"Say please."

She giggled. "Please, Brad."

"What do you want?"

"You're such a tease! I want your big cock inside me now, Brad. Please."

"That's better." He plunged inside her, enjoying the sound she made as he went deep. "Damn, you feel good. So nice and tight..."

"Oh...Brad...you feel so good...Fuck me harder..." She grabbed his ass and pulled him deeper. *I was right. She's not such a good girl. Thank God for that.*

He looked down, watching her as he thrust harder and harder. Then he saw her face. Except it wasn't Sheila's. It was Karen's face. The Ice Queen. Her pale blue eyes taunted him as if to say, "See you can't even fuck anyone else without thinking about me."

Damn it.

His mind drifted as he thought of what it would feel like to have Karen underneath him. It pissed him off and aroused him at the same time. He didn't want to think about her unless he absolutely had to. It was enough that he had to deal with her five days a week. He didn't need to be plagued with thoughts of her on the weekend, too. But, he couldn't help but imagine what she would be like in bed. *I bet she'd be a handful.* The idea excited him more than he cared to admit.

Sheila's moans brought him back to the present. He flipped her over so she was on all fours and then plunged into her again, making her call out. Reaching around her waist, he began making small circles on her clit, which only made her cry out louder. He sped up the circles, using more pressure, and thrusted harder until she whimpered.

"Brad! You're making me come, Brad! Oh, yes...*yes*! *yes*!" He loved that sound, loved the way she moved, the way her entire body vibrated as she exploded around him. He came with her, then pulled out slowly as she collapsed into a heap on the bed, the sheets now damp.

TWO

Karen poured more vanilla creamer into her coffee. *Well, look at him strutting in here. He looks different today. I wonder what he did this weekend.*

"Good morning, Karen. How are you?" Brad kept up his happy-guy strut as he came into the break room.

"I'm great. You're chipper this morning. I take it you had a good weekend?"

He nodded as he poured himself a cup. "Yes, very." He sighed. "Just what I needed."

"Good, because you have several messages waiting for you. Oh, and just a head's up. Mr. Jensen called. They sent the call to me by mistake. He doesn't sound happy." She turned on her heel and started to make her exit.

"Oh he's fine. I'll talk to him."

He's completely unfazed. What the hell? Karen stopped in her tracks and turned back around. "I don't know; he sounded pretty upset. You know he's temperamental. You were able to smooth talk him before, but how many times do you think you can do that?"

Brad laughed. "He'll be fine. This is just a stressful situation for him. He's not going to fire me. He just needs to vent and let it out then he'll feel better. Didn't they teach you in law school that we have to be their therapist, too?"

Karen shrugged. "If you say so." As she walked down the hall, it hit her: *He had sex this weekend! That is the only explanation. Well, I wonder who she was –* She slammed the door to her office. *What the hell do I care?* She shook her head, trying to rid her mind of the image of Brad having sex.

At exactly 5:30, Karen shut down her computer. She had managed to avoid Brad most of the day, not wanting to see anymore of his perky I-Just-Got-Laid face. Could he make it any more obvious? *You'd think by his cheesy demeanor it was the first time he had sex. How pathetic. Oh, the young ones.*

***

Pippa's was packed that night. It was Karen's favorite after work hangout because it was quiet, dark and the food was excellent. A man who looked to be in his mid-twenties was perched on a small stage bathed in blue light playing acoustic guitar. He was usually playing when Karen stopped in. Tonight he was doing Kings of Leon covers. His velvety voice was soft and soothing, low and soulful. Every couple of songs, he would look over at Karen and smile shyly and wink. The powdery blue stage lights shone on his light brown hair and above his head, she could see dust particles float through the air.

Karen had invited her friend Hailey out for a drink when she decided she wasn't quite ready to go home. She could always count on her friend to not only cheer her up, but to be brutally honest and give her much-needed advice. Hailey had been two years ahead of Karen in law school and already owned her own small firm just outside of Boston. With caramel skin, black hair, and bright green eyes, she was an exotic beauty. When the two were together, people tended to think they were sisters, except that Karen had snow-white skin.

"I just didn't feel like heading home yet. Thanks for meeting me." Karen took a sip of her scotch.

Hailey leaned forward, her green eyes sparkling. "Of course, anytime. I was glad to hear from you. You're always too busy to get together."

"Yeah, I know. I'm sorry about that. I don't know how you do it."

She shrugged. "I don't sleep much. Are you still seeing Chris?"

Karen sighed. "No. Well, I mean I saw him last week. It's just...ugh...he's so sweet, but..."

"He still hopeless in the sack?"

Karen looked around the bar, met the singer's eyes and he smiled again as he began strumming the opening chords to Use Somebody. "Oh, Hailey. Yes. It's terrible. I'm losing hope."

"Then end it. I don't get it."

"Yeah, I know. I was just hoping I could teach him, but he doesn't seem to get it. He's clueless and I'm getting impatient. I know that's not the most important thing, but –"

"But terrible sex is unacceptable, Karen. You're better off going solo. At least you'll get off."

"True. I mean, he doesn't seem to understand female anatomy at all. It's just a turn-off."

Hailey laughed. "Well, there are plenty of fish in the sea, so don't waste your time!"

"You're right. I was just hoping this would work out. He's such a great guy, other than the sex. Damn it. I just can't do it anymore."

"Then, don't." Hailey took a sip of her Syrah. "Hey! Don't you have a cute new associate at the office? Brad something?"

"How do you know about him?"

"Amy told me. She showed me his picture on the company website. He's hot, Karen. How do you get any work done with him around?"

"Seriously, Hailey. He's cute, but too young. You know I like the older ones."

"Yeah and that's gross. You should give him a chance."

Karen leaned forward, her eyes widened. "Give him a chance? We work together. That could get really messy. So, no, not going to happen."

Hailey looked off into the distance. "Hmm...*I* wouldn't mind getting messy with him."

"You do like the pretty ones."

Hailey sighed and gave a wistful smile. "He *is* gorgeous."

Later that night, Karen laid in bed wishing she could fall asleep. Her hands began slowly drifting down her stomach, drawing wide circles with her nails, traveling down to the top of her black lace panties, down to her upper thigh. Making her way back up to the delicate lace, tracing the pattern with her fingertips, she felt her nipples harden. Pushing up her matching lace camisole, she lightly caressed her hardened peaks with the palm of her left hand, slowly moving from one to the other. With her right hand, she grazed over the patch of lace between her legs, feeling the fabric dampen. Pinching her nipple harder now, she felt a tingle go from the tips of her fingers to the base of her spine like a gentle current of electricity. Her hips moved in response as she quickened the pace, then impatiently squirmed her way out of the restrictive lace, kicking the panties off her feet and onto the floor. Her hand found her wet center again, this time slick with her juices, the sensations intensifying as she pressed harder, making small circles. She was getting close already.

The only thing that would feel better is his tongue. Brad's face appeared in her mind, his sparkling deep brown eyes, his angular jaw, his five o'clock shadow, his soft jet-black hair. He always wore a suit and tie, and as the day wore on, he would take off his jacket and walk around in his crisp white button down shirt. The way the fabric grazed his skin, she could tell he was muscular. She imagined unbuttoning his shirt, peeling it off, then unbuckling his belt, unzipping his pants, pulling them down...He would push her onto the bed and climb on top of her, pinning her arms above her head, as he slowly tortured and teased her, sucking her nipples, then working his way down, licking her juices, flicking and sucking her. She felt her body clench and as her back arched, she rubbed harder and faster until she felt her torso lift off the bed as her legs and toes stiffen, the muscles inside her contract, an explosion starting under her fingers as she saw Brad's eyes boring into hers, telling her to come for him, a naughty smirk on his beautiful face. She convulsed as her hips bucked and circled as she exploded and saw white bursts of light under her eyelids.

She couldn't move. Every muscle was limp and useless. Wiping her forehead, she sighed and stared at the ceiling. Goosebumps appeared on her skin as an aftershock came over her and she shivered, pulling the plush white comforter over her naked, damp body.

"Just what I needed," she said softly to her empty room. She breathed a contented sigh and rolled to her side, feeling drowsy.

Her eyes popped open when she remembered the face that was in her mind when she climaxed. She felt her face flush. *What the hell? I don't even like him that way.* But she smiled in spite of herself when she thought about the way he had refused to pour her coffee. At least he has some backbone. She would have been disappointed had he actually done it.

***

Half sitting on the edge of her desk, she bit into a Snickers bar. She didn't eat junk food often, but she kept an emergency stash in her bottom desk drawer for times like these.

Brad was walking down the hall and stopped just in front of her office as he spoke with one of the paralegals. Karen studied the way he stood as he listened to her: his head cocked to one side, his eyes narrowed, and a slight smile rested on his face. Today he was wearing a light blue dress shirt, a navy blue tie with pale blue stripes and black dress pants that hugged his toned behind nicely. When he shifted his weight from one foot to the other, she was mesmerized by the way his body moved, even in this slight movement. Then, suddenly his eyes met hers and the corners of his mouth lifted and his eyes sparkled, seemingly saying, "I caught you."

Damn it. She quickly looked away.

"What's wrong with you?" Julia, Karen's assistant, asked. When exactly Julia had walked in the room, Karen had no idea.

"Where did you come from?"

Julia laughed. "Too distracted by the new eye candy? I walked in about a minute ago."

"Eye candy? I've seen better. I'm just keeping an eye on him, making sure he's up to par."

"You were scowling, so I'm guessing it's not good?"

"No, he's okay so far." She stood up and adjusted her blouse, smoothed her skirt. "I don't know, I just feel restless and irritable."

"Maybe you're PMS'ing."

"No, it's not time for that."

"Is it a guy?"

"Please. Like I'd let some doofus get to me."

"Karen, you're human. It's okay if you care about someone."

"Yeah, well I don't have time to care. I'm okay being single. In fact, I'm really good at it and I plan to keep it that way. Every man I've dated has been threatened by my success anyway."

Julia raised her eyebrows.

Karen shrugged. "Believe it or not, it's true.

And if that sounds egotistical, so be it. It's just how it is. They want a sweet little wifey to cook them dinner at night and suck their dick. Sure, they want her to be smart, but not *too* smart. They want her to be ambitious, but not *too* ambitious. They are insecure little mama's boys who need the woman to ask him to open the jar of pickles because, oh!" She mimed holding a jar and trying to unscrew the lid. "I just can't! But thank God I have you to do it for me!"

Julia's laughter could be heard throughout the office. "Jesus, Karen!" She grabbed Karen's coffee mug and set it aside. "Enough for you!"

"What? I'm serious. You can't tell me everything I said isn't true. Every woman knows it." She defiantly grabbed her coffee mug and placed it next to her.

"Yes, to an extent it's true. For some men. Not all."

Karen huffed. "For most. At least from my vantage point."

"Okay, well, you need a super successful guy, then. Because most other men will be threatened by you. But there are men out there who won't be. You just have to find them."

Karen gave a dramatic shiver and walked around the desk to her chair. "Ugh. I don't want to *find* them. It's too much work. I have enough work to do. Finding a boyfriend should be easy."

Julia sat in the chair by the window, stared out for a moment. "It can be a lot of work. Which is why I have two cats, no husband. But that's a different story. You are absolutely gorgeous, Karen, and on top of everything else, that's even more threatening to them."

Karen sighed, shook her head. "It's crazy. Nothing makes sense. Everything you think you know is wrong. You think, if I'm beautiful, successful, intelligent, men will flock to me. But, the last two men I dated, who I was madly in love with, they went on to marry and when I saw their wives, I just didn't get it. Maybe she's a great person, but she's just so...plain Jane! Take my ex's wife, Sarah. I met her a few months ago. She was very average looking, not a toned muscle on her body, sporting a mom hairdo, wearing a cardigan and khaki pants." She laughed. "I was just...wow, okay, if that's what you want. And it's not just the appearance. I met her, and she had no personality! She smiled the whole time and was sugary sweet, but I felt like I was talking to a mannequin. She just looked right through me, didn't seem to understand a word I was saying. Just had those big, round vacant eyes." Karen widened her eyes to mimic Sarah.

Julia laughed. "Trust me, I know. I see women like that with hot guys all the time. I don't get it. There must be something we don't know."

"Right? I want to pull her aside and say, 'Alright, sister, tell me. Do you give the best BJ's in the world? Do you have no gag reflex or something? Do you swing naked from the chandelier? Do you cook dinner in a lace thong and high heels? Tell me your secret!' One day I'm going to just ask. I can't stand it. I have to know."

"Please do!" Julia said, leaning forward in her chair, laughing. "And then spread the word so we can even the playing field."

"Oh, I will. This is a mystery I will solve. You can count on it." Karen looked up at the wall, an antique brass clock was perched above the doorframe, ticking quietly. "Is that thing accurate?"

Julia looked down at her watch. "Yes, it's eleven."

"Okay, let's get to it. We've already wasted enough time discussing the eighth wonder of the world."

"Agreed. I'm almost done with Mr. Thompson's property settlement agreement. I'll email it to you as soon as I'm finished."

"Perfect. Oh, and could you send Brad in here if you see him?"

"Will do."

Ten minutes later, Brad walked in. He looked dashing as always, a smug smile on his chiseled face, his brown eyes sparkling. Was he still gloating about catching her staring? He leaned against the doorframe and crossed his arms in front of his chest. "It's because they want a mother for their children. A woman whose sole focus is on the family."

"I'm sorry?"

"To answer your question from a man's perspective. It's because they want a simple woman. They want her to be a devoted wife and mother, be completely focused on taking care of the house and children. They may be threatened by a more ambitious woman, but it's more because they fear she won't want to focus so much on family. But you're right, a lot of men want the woman to be intelligent only to a certain level. More than that, and it makes them feel insecure. Not all men are like that, of course."

She raised an eyebrow as she leaned back in her chair and crossed her arms over her chest. "You were eavesdropping?"

"Not intentionally. I could hear you two down the hallway." Brad cocked his head to the side, motioning to the left.

"I doubt we were talking that loud. You should spend more time working and less time listening to others' conversations."

Brad chuckled. "I was working, Miss Sanders. But I could hear you."

"So we were interrupting your work?"

He appeared to be repressing another laugh, which pissed Karen off. *Why was he so cocky all of a sudden?* "No, no. It was an interesting conversation, so I didn't mind hearing it."

"Well, you're in luck, because I need you to stay late tonight. You will get a chance to catch up on all the work you missed while Julia and I were so rudely distracting you."

She caught a flicker of a scowl, but he quickly hid it. *Good. He needs to be taken down a notch. Harvard or not, no one walks in here and thinks they are going to put me in my place.*

"No problem." He smiled.

She was disappointed. It would have been fun if he had tried to fight her on this. Tell her he had plans, he couldn't stay.

"Good. I need your help with a few things and I'm sure you need to get some things done, too."

"I do, actually. Good call. I should get ahead on some things." He started to walk away but turned back to her. "Do you need anything else?"

"No, that's all."

He gave a quick nod and breezed out of the room as if he had not a care in the world.

She laughed quietly, shaking her head. *Who the hell does he think he is? He's a baby lawyer. This is his first job and he comes in acting all smug, like he's in charge. He has a lot to learn. Good thing I'm here to teach him.* She shook her mouse, waking her computer up and decided to tackle her inbox. *Maybe by ten o'clock tonight, he will have learned.*

THREE

At half past six, she picked up her phone and dialed 142.

"This is Brad."

"I need you in here, please."

"Sure, be right there."

She had asked him to stay late under the pretense of needing his help, but she was really trying to determine just how smart he really was. As it turned out, he was quite intelligent and even crafty when it came to dealing with clients and their angry soon-to-be exes. Later in the evening, she decided to find out how he had dealt with one of the firm's most challenging cases.

"So, what's happening with Mr. Jensen?"

"We had a meeting today with his ex, Stacey, and her attorney—"

"Who is Stacey's attorney?"

"Sylvia Woodsen."

Karen's eyes widened. "Sylvia? She's a shark. Good luck with that one." She chuckled.

"Really? Well, after I mentioned Stacey's past alcohol problem and the fact that she had tried to leave her husband with the children ten years ago, Sylvia pulled Stacey aside and left the room. When they came back ten minutes later, Sylvia advised us that Stacey had agreed to share custody, giving Carl every other week and three weeks in the summer with the children."

"Oh, shit."

Brad laughed. "Yeah, Sylvia was pissed but there was nothing she could do about it. Stacey had failed to mention her little alcoholic episode to her own attorney. She had even spent a couple weeks in rehab years ago. So there's documentation. No judge would give her full custody."

"No, he wouldn't. Well, good job, Brad."

"Thank you."

"Now." She started searching the top of her desk. "Where is the Muniz file?"

She caught a whiff of his cologne as he reached over, picked up the file and handed it to her. For a brief second, their faces were an inch apart and she was transfixed by the deep pools of brown looking directly at her. It was almost too intimate and she felt an urge to lean in and kiss him. He quickly straightened back up, but not before she saw his smirk. Had he noticed her reaction to him? Surely not. The guy can't read minds.

When he leaned back to his chair, he asked, "So, why are you single, if you don't mind my asking? I mean, I find it hard to believe that every guy you've met is scared off by your career."

She laughed. "You want to talk about this again?"

He shrugged. "I just don't get it. Not all men are like that."

"Oh, really?" She put down the file. "Let me guess: you're one of those men who isn't threatened by a strong, successful woman?"

He met her gaze. "I find it to be a major turn-on actually."

She huffed and looked away. "Yeah. That's what they all say. After a while, the truth comes out."

He paused for a beat. "Well, apparently you've never been with a real man, Karen."

She laughed. "Oh, please. You are really cute, you know that, Brad? I have to hand it to you, confidence is attractive."

His face turned serious. "You are really condescending to me, you know that, Karen?"

"I'm not condescending. I'm hard on you because I have to be. It's my job, Brad. It's nothing personal."

"It sure feels personal to me. And I don't appreciate being spoken to that way. So, stop talking down to me."

Karen laughed and stood up. She walked around and leaned against the front of the desk facing him. "Or what?"

He stood and walked towards her. "I may be new here but I deserve respect and I will get it."

"You have to earn it just like everyone else. So, suck it up."

"You know, if we weren't at work, this situation would be entirely different. You wouldn't have gotten away with treating me as you have for so long. I'd have put an end to it long ago."

"Oh, I bet," she said.

He stepped closer. "You're not really this mean, are you? You just act like an ice queen so you don't look weak."

"You have some nerve, don't you?" She squared her shoulders and looked up at him. She began to turn but he gently grabbed her arm to stop her.

She looked down at his hand in surprise. "Don't touch me."

He didn't let go. "You don't mean that."

As she looked into his eyes, she felt powerless to look away. And she felt the familiar ache she always experienced when he was near. His close proximity, his soapy, woodsy scent and his intense gaze were unnerving.

"Brad," she said softly.

He leaned in and kissed her cheek. "That's what I thought. I catch you staring at me all the time. Are you going to deny that?"

"I'm just keeping an eye on you," she said. Even that didn't sound convincing to her.

He smiled but stayed silent a moment. "You're stubborn," he said finally. "I can feel the effect I have on you. And I'd be lying if I said you didn't have the same effect on me."

"That may be true, but we work together, so this is inappropriate."

"You're admitting it? Good, we're getting somewhere."

Karen bit her lip and looked away. She had no idea how to respond.

"This is inappropriate, but no one else is here right now. Everyone has left for the night and it's just us." He took her chin in his hand and lifted her face to his.

She pulled away and walked over to the other side of the room. "Brad, this is just. . ."

Watching as he walked towards her, she thought of how much he looked like an animal stalking his prey. She couldn't control her reaction. Her skin felt like it was catching fire and she felt her panties slowly getting wet. So many emotions churned inside her, confusing her. She was afraid to let down her guard for even a split second, for fear that he may take over her completely and there would be no turning back. But, this fire burning under her skin and this desire, this longing was almost uncontrollable.

Her heart accelerated as he stood in front of her, his face less than in inch away from hers. She could feel his body heat but resisted the urge to lean into him. She didn't have to resist long, because he pressed his body into hers and she could feel his erection against her skirt.

In one swift motion, he took her hands and pulled them over head and pinned them against the wall. "Tell me to stop," he whispered in her ear.

She felt her knees go weak and her heart accelerate again. He placed a foot between her high heels and gently nudged to force her to spread her legs. He pressed into her harder.

"Tell me, Karen. You're the boss. Tell me to stop and I will."

"Brad, I. . ." She looked away.

He wasn't having that. He held her face in his hands and forced her to meet his gaze. "You have to tell me one way or another," he said softly. "Because if you don't stop me..." He kissed the side of her neck, sending chills down her spine. "Tell me to leave the room and I will," he said, continuing his wicked assault on her neck and down to her collarbone.

She was silent as he continued planting kisses, working his way up and down her neck, his hands grazing along the sides of her breasts and down to her waist and hips. It felt so good and for a moment she was lost in the sensations she was feeling all over her body. She wanted him. Wanted to rip his clothes off and touch every inch of that hard, muscular body. But, her pride wouldn't let her succumb to her lust. *I can't have sex with him! What am I thinking? No, this has to stop.*

Using both hands, she pushed him away.

He took a couple steps back and watched her. "You were enjoying that."

"We can't, Brad." She smoothed her hair and adjusted her skirt. "Now, I think you should go."

"We can't, or you won't because you're afraid you might enjoy it?"

She sighed loudly. "Brad—"

He laughed. "I know, I know. I get it." He picked up his briefcase and started towards the door. "Goodnight, Karen."

FOUR

She plopped down into her chair and stared blankly into space. *What is wrong with me? Well, I'm glad I stopped it when I did.* But her body was still buzzing with arousal and she felt the familiar ache down low that wouldn't go away. She decided to make a point to be extra professional from then on, even a little cold, especially around Brad. He could not start thinking this was going to be a regular occurrence. It didn't matter that she was attracted to him; she had a reputation to uphold and a career to build. If she slept with Brad and word got out, she'd never be taken seriously. It was hard enough for a woman to make her name as a lawyer; it was still such a boy's club that she had to claw her way to the top and fight every step of the way to gain the respect she deserved. She couldn't let some young newbie ruin her chances of being the kick-ass lawyer she was meant to be. A few more years and she would start her own firm, call the shots.

***

"So, next up, let's see..." Ethan Marks, the senior attorney and partner, looked down at his notes. The entire staff was gathered in the conference room for their monthly meeting. Karen had arrived at work early that morning to prepare and to secure the seat next to Ethan. She knew from experience that where you sat in a meeting made an impact on the way you were perceived. Sitting at the head of the table with the other partners was absolutely essential. "We'd like to welcome Brad Thomas, our newest addition to Marks, Smith and Sanders." He motioned to Brad, who stood and smiled, giving a quick wave to the rest of the staff. "I know you've already met everyone on the team, but we'd like to officially welcome you. I've been hearing great things. Isn't that right, Karen? You've been working closely with him over the last couple of weeks to get him acquainted with the office and how we operate."

"Yes, I have and he's doing quite well." She glanced at Brad and forced a polite smile.

"Thank you, Karen." He smiled back but looked away quickly, as if to dismiss her opinion as inconsequential.

During the remainder of the meeting, Brad did not make eye contact with her once. It seemed as if he was purposely ignoring her. *Oh, so that's how he wants to play it. Well, that's fine with me. The less interaction with him, the better.*

***

She glanced up from her desk to see Brad walking down the hall.

"Oh, Brad?" She called out. *Let's see him try to ignore me now.*

He stopped and peeked his head in. "Yeah?"

"Where are you going for lunch?"

"I'm actually meeting a client today."

"Great, so while you're out could you get me—"

"I won't be able to. Sorry, Karen." He smiled and walked away.

She felt her face warm with anger. *Who the hell does he think he is?*

A couple of hours later, Brad sauntered back into the office grinning like an idiot. Ethan stopped him in the hallway just outside Karen's office and gave him a loud pat on the back.

"Brad! I hear you recruited another client today. You're learning fast, son."

"Jesus," Karen muttered under her breath. *Yeah, he's learned how to kiss ass quickly.* The senior attorney loved him. She knew she shouldn't feel jealous; she had proven herself long ago and had great working relationships with the attorneys. But, Brad was moving much faster when it came to earning their respect. They had been much harder on her when she first started at the firm. It took years before they treated her like an equal. Brad was already getting literal pats on the back and 'atta –boys almost daily.

Brad's face lit up like a Christmas tree and his brown eyes sparkled in the light from the sconce on the wall. "Yes, Shandra Johnson. I'm loving it. Thank you so much for the opportunity, sir."

Karen laughed out loud before she caught herself. *Is he for real? Why doesn't he just get down on his knees now? Dear God.* She shook her head.

Both men glanced over. "Everything okay, Karen?" Ethan looked concerned.

"Oh, yes. Just fine. Excuse me," she said, and picked up her phone and dialed Julia.

"Yes?"

"Could you grab me a coffee please? And maybe add some Kahlua?"

Julia laughed. "That bad, huh? On my way."

Later, as she was checking her email, Karen glanced at the clock. 4:00. She still had so much work to do; she was going to be here all night. Unless she had some help. Julia had left early for an appointment. The only other person who could help her with this would be Brad. Reluctantly, she dialed Brad's extension.

When he picked up, she said, "I need your help tonight, please."

"Oh, Karen, you know what? I'm sorry but I can't. I have plans."

"Well, cancel them. You know that big client you just landed? Well," she continued without letting him respond. "she's going to be more work. You're going to have to research the—"

"The pre-nup. I know, I'm working on it. I've got it handled, Karen. There's no need to worry."

Karen paused. "Are you aware of how time sensitive this is? This needs to be prepared by the end of the week."

"Of course. I'm almost finished with it. I'll wrap it up tomorrow."

"You're almost finished? I highly doubt that, Brad. I don't think you realize what is involved. But, sure, finish it tomorrow."

"Sure thing. Have a good night, Karen."

"Same to you," she said before slamming the phone down. *Wait. It's 4:00. Is he leaving?* She shrugged. *That's okay. He'll be here until midnight tomorrow.*

FIVE

The next day, Karen saw Brad come in early, but he didn't come out of his office for lunch until 3:00. She stood from her desk and met him in the hallway.

"Busy today?"

"Yes, very. But, I'll get it done. Not a problem." He smiled and began to walk away.

Just then, Ethan walked over to them. "How's the Johnson case?"

"It's going well," Brad answered brightly.

"Really? Well, good. From what I hear, it's a heavy load. Lots of complications."

"There are, but—"

"Why don't you have one of us take a look later? I'm sure you've got it, but this is a lot to take on so early in your career."

Karen looked at Ethan. "It is pretty intense.

I'd be happy to look over it later." *Two can play the kiss up game.* Then, smiling at Brad, she said, "Why don't you stop by my office later, say around five?"

She noticed Brad square his shoulders. "Of course. That's a good idea."

***

Brad sighed. "What page are you on?"

"Fifteen. We're almost done, Brad." She smiled. "This is why I asked you to stay late the other night."

"Oh, I'm not tired. It's just a little tedious, but I'm fine. I have stamina." The way he said it sounded vaguely sexual. Or maybe it was just that everything sounded that way when you were sexually deprived.

"I'm glad to hear it."

"Are you?" He gave her a wicked grin.

Now she was sure he was flirting. "Sure, Brad."

He laughed. "Lighten up. When was the last time you went out and had a good time?"

"Pretty recently, but thanks for your concern. I'm too busy to go out all the time. Now, can we focus on this so we're not here all night?"

"There it is again."

"What?"

"You're being condescending again." He paused. "I don't think you even realize it."

Karen sighed. "Okay, Brad. Whatever you say. I'm too tired to argue. I'm grabbing some coffee, I'll be back," she said as she stood up from her chair and stretched.

She was shocked when Brad stood in front of

her blocking her path.

"Excuse me, Brad." She tried to walk around him but he stopped her.

Just as she was about to make a sarcastic comment, she looked up and forgot her words when she met his eyes. They were alight with humor, twinkling in the white light of the computer screen. He stepped closer and she felt that familiar warmth begin to spread like flames at her feet drifting up her legs, to her hips, all the way up to her face. It felt as if someone turned on the heat in the building.

"Unless all of that is just a cover." Brad touched her hand.

"A cover for what?" She felt a chill where his hand had touched hers.

He grinned again. "I think you know."

She said nothing. What was there to say? As much as she hated to admit it, she was attracted to him. Even the fact that he kissed up and was quickly becoming the golden boy of the office; it pissed her off and turned her on at the same time. It was confusing. She simultaneously wanted to slap him and kiss him. *Maybe both.*

His eyebrows shot up. "What's that coy smile for?"

Without letting her answer, he touched her cheek and leaned closer. Their lips were now an inch apart. It was decision time. *Damn it.* A second later, she had made her decision. Her lips parted and she met his. *I'm going to regret this.* She felt his tongue swirl inside her mouth and the heat taking over her body.

He used his body to gently push her to her the wall. She was pinned as his tongue continued its magic and she felt herself grow aroused at the thought of what else his tongue could do. His hips pressed into hers and she felt his hard length against her skirt.

"Do you want me to stop?"

"No..." she whispered.

"Good, because I really don't want to." He brought her arms down to her sides. "Now, keep your arms where they are and don't move." Starting at her neck, he began planting soft kisses, then took her face in his hands and kissed her lips, pushing his tongue into her mouth, caressing her tongue with his. When he pulled away, she whimpered. He ripped her blouse open, sending buttons flying to the floor. He pulled it completely off, then pulled her bra straps down until her breasts were exposed. Her nipples hardened in the chilly office air. He watched her eyes as he pinched them.

"Do you like that?"

"Yes..."

"What about this?" He bent forward and began swirling his tongue around her nipple, stopping occasionally to flick it with his tongue. There was no use trying to resist him any longer. She was powerless. She arched her back, pushing her breasts out to him.

"God, yes. I love that, Brad."

"I bet you're getting wet for me, aren't you?"

"Mmm..." she moaned. "I think so..."

"I'm going to have to make sure," he said. Kneeling down, he pushed up her skirt and touched the thin strip of lace between her legs. He growled. "Mmm...your panties are so wet, Karen. You're such a bad girl, aren't you?"

"Yes..."

"No, tell me you're a bad girl."

"I'm a bad girl."

"Yes, you are. And not just because your panties are wet. But because you've been disrespectful to me. I think you need to learn a lesson."

She gazed down at him now on his knees between her legs. "Brad, you know I'm just doing—"

"Yeah, yeah, you're just doing your job. I know. But, you take it too far. I'm going to balance this relationship a little."

He pulled her panties down and tossed them across the room. He then unzipped her skirt and pulled it down. She was now naked except for her high heels.

He touched the patent leather of her shoes. "We'll leave these on." Taking her hand, he led her to the desk. "Lie on the desk and spread your legs."

When she complied, he studied her a moment. She felt so vulnerable and exposed and it turned her on. Although, she still wasn't sure what Brad meant by her needing to learn a lesson.

He walked around the desk, stopping to play with her nipples, pinching them, biting them, then walked down the end and pulled her legs open wider, touched her wet center. She trembled and let out a small gasp. "I bet you never thought you'd be lying naked on your desk with your legs spread wide open for me, did you?"

"No," she whimpered.

He kept touching her, watching her reactions. "Beautiful," he said.

"Please," she said. "I want you."

"I know you do. But I'm in charge now. So, you'll do as I say. Do you understand?"

"Yes."

"Good." He ran his hands from her breasts down to the apex of her thighs. "I want to taste this." Leaning down, he began to tease and lick, stopping to flick her clit and then sucking it.

"Oh, Brad, that feels so good." She felt her legs tremble. The man knew what he was doing.

He put a finger inside her and began thrusting as he swirled his tongue around her clit.

She moaned and began moving her hips.

"Don't move."

She stopped moving but it was so hard to control it. She couldn't believe she was already close to climaxing. It normally took several minutes.

"Good girl. Who's in charge here?"

"You are."

"Good. You're getting close, aren't you?"

"Mmm....yes...so close...please, Brad."

"Please what?"

"Please make me come."

"Oh, I will. But I want an apology. You have been very mean and disrespectful to me."

She started to close her legs. *No, we are not doing this.* But he pushed them back apart. She squirmed. "Never. I told you, I'm doing what I have to do."

He started to stand up. "Okay, then."

"No, wait."

He stared down at her. "What?"

"Okay, okay. Please, Brad. Don't tease me like that."

"Why? Is it mean and cold? Selfish, inconsiderate?"

"Fuck. I hate you."

"No, you don't. You like me but you try to

41

hide it under that bitchy exterior. I could see right through it, though. Let's start with something easier then. Tell me what you were thinking earlier today when I caught you staring at me."

"Oh, please. I was just lost in thought."

He surprised her by laughing. "Right." He trailed his fingertips along the inside of her legs, starting at her ankle and working his way up to her thighs. "You are so stubborn."

"I want you."

"Is that what you were thinking?"

"Something like that, yes."

"You were fantasizing about me?"

She said nothing. He reached up and flicked her clit a few times with his finger. "Were you?"

"Yes!" She squirmed. "I was, okay? What's your point?"

"Do you want me to make you come?"

"Yes."

"So," he said, leaning forward and licking her clit once more, putting two fingers inside her. "All you need to do is say one thing to me and I'll let you come."

He increased the pressure with his tongue and the speed of his thrusting fingers, then suddenly stopped.

She slammed her hand down on the desk. "Okay! Damn it, Brad. I'm sorry."

"Sorry for what?" He started fingering her again slowly.

"I'm sorry I was so mean to you. I was disrespectful to you. It won't happen again."

"Promise?"

"God, yes!"

He laughed and increased the speed again, pressing and swirling his tongue against her swollen clit. "Glad to hear it. Now, come for me, Miss Sanders."

She felt the wicked tingle start at the tip of his tongue and begin to travel deep inside her. Arching her back, she felt the spasm start inside her and explode as her body trembled and a chill traveled the length of her spine.

"Yes! Oh, God, yes, Brad!"

She fell back onto the desk as she caught her breath.

"That's a beautiful sight," he said as he began unbuckling his belt.

She watched him pull off his pants and unbutton his shirt. He had the most beautiful body she had ever seen. She sucked in a breath when he pulled off his boxers. He was massive. He noticed her reaction and smirked. "You like?"

"Yes," she said. "Give it to me."

"So demanding. Don't forget who's in charge right now." He walked around to the side of the desk. "Open your mouth."

She did as she was told and he eased himself into her mouth. "That's right. Now, suck."

As she sucked and swirled her tongue around him, he reached down and pinched her nipples, making her groan. Then, he reached farther down and played some more. She spread her legs wider to give him better access. When she looked up at him, she noticed his expression: cocky and triumphant. It made her a little angry that she had given into him so easily. Now, he would think he was in charge. But her anger had a surprising effect: it aroused her even more and she was close to climax from his skilled fingers.

He pushed himself into her and she cried out.

"That's right. You like it, don't you?"

"Yes, Brad."

"And I'm going to give it to you hard." He thrust inside her slowly at first, then sped up and pushed into her roughly. She could feel herself being stretched and it was the most delicious feeling in the world. After a few minutes, he picked her up and turned her over so she was bent over the desk. He plunged into her again, holding onto her hips. Then he gave her a slap on her behind.

"What's that for?" she asked, breathlessly.

He spanked her again, five more times.

"Ow! Brad!"

"That's for making me get you lunch the other day. I'm not your assistant."

"I do that with all the new—"

He slapped her behind again, harder this time.

"Okay, okay! I'm sorry. I won't do it again."

"Oh, I know you won't."

"You're really cocky, you know that?"

He didn't answer, just kept thrusting harder and harder until she felt the build up again. "Come with me, Karen."

They shared a simultaneous climax on her large mahogany desk and Karen collapsed, exhausted, resting her cheek against the cold surface. Her legs were trembling from holding the position for so long.

She heard Brad's quiet chuckle. "You okay?"

"Mmm..." she mumbled.

He scooped her up as if she were light as a feather and sat her on the black leather couch. She closed her eyes and relaxed for a moment. She jumped when she heard Brad's voice. "That is a beautiful image."

"What?" She rubbed her eyes and looked around.

"You in nothing but your fuck-me heels. I've been wanting to see you like this for a while, I won't lie."

"My fuck-me heels?" She laughed.

"That's what they are. You've been wearing them a lot lately."

"Well, I like them."

"So do I."

She yawned then looked at the clock on the wall. "It's late."

"It sure is. Here," he handed her the now destroyed blouse along with the rest of her clothing.

She laughed again. "What am I supposed to do with this? The buttons are gone." She kicked off her heels to put on her panties and skirt, then put on her bra, wrapping her open blouse around her torso.

"My bad." He pulled his jacket off the chair and wrapped it around her. "Now you're decent."

"So chivalrous!"

"I can be. Let me walk you out to your car."

SIX

Back at her house, Karen stood in front of the stove, waiting for her teapot to whistle so she could have her nightly chamomile tea. Stretching her neck, she wondered briefly why she was so sore and then remembered the events of the night. Sleeping with the new attorney – as hot as he was – may have been a huge mistake. She knew Brad wouldn't tell anyone, but if word got out, it would be a disaster.

I can't do that again. She poured the hot water over the teabag in her mug. He had seduced her and she had not only let him, but begged him. She shuddered. Surrendering control to a man was not something she was prepared to do. Not today. Not ever. Especially a man she worked with. If word got out that she was screwing her co-worker, it would soil her reputation, diminish her credibility. She had to fight hard enough as it was to be taken seriously. Even in this day and age, she had still been treated like a secretary when she had first started at the firm right out of college. That didn't last long, though, because she quickly showed them that she demanded respect and was a force to be reckoned with. She had sacrificed and stayed late every night for a year, having no social life. Last Thanksgiving, she had dinner with her family on Thursday, but on Friday, had gone to the office and worked ten hours while everyone else was home. She was not about to let all that hard work she had invested go down the drain. Not for Mr. Brad Thomas, newly minted esquire.

"Look, we can't do this again. It's not a good idea," Karen said, backing away. Brad had waltzed into her office at lunchtime, closed the door, shut the blinds and picked her up from her chair and pulled her into a long embrace, kissing her until she was breathless.

"Says who? We are both adults and it is no one's business but ours." He pushed a stray piece of hair out of her face. "Do you think I'd tell anyone? Go around bragging? I'm not like that, Karen."

"Maybe you're not. But, I can't risk it."

"You can't risk it or I'm not worth it?"

"Oh, God. Brad, that's not what I mean." She pushed his hands aside and started to walk towards the door. "We need to open this door. It looks suspicious already."

He laughed. "So paranoid."

She wheeled around and stared him down for a moment. "Are you serious? Brad, think. It's pretty obvious —"

He put his hands up in surrender. "Okay, okay! I understand." He walked towards her. "So, let's not do this in the office. Let's see each other outside of work."

She sighed. "I don't know..."

"You're worried and I get that. But I – I want to keep seeing you. So, let me take you out tonight."

"Tonight is no good—"

He smiled. "Okay. When is good?"

"Maybe Friday."

"Perfect. I'll pick you up at eight. Wear that white clingy dress with your red fuck-me heels." He gave a male grunt of appreciation. "Please," he added with a sheepish smile.

She smiled back in spite of herself.

"Text me your address," he said as he opened the office door and walked out.

Julia walked in at the same moment and looked questioningly at Brad's back as he walked down the hall. "Is he strutting?"

"What?"

"Oh, yeah, he's strutting. What just happened?"

Karen made sure to look confused. "Nothing happened. He always struts. Haven't you noticed?"

Julia gave her a "stop-bullshitting-me" look.

"He was just gloating over landing yet another client. He's getting cocky."

"He's yummy, so he can be as cocky as he wants..."

"Julia!"

"What?" Julia sat in front of Karen's desk. "Oh, come on. He's hot so stop acting like you haven't noticed."

"Yeah, he's cute, but not my type."

"Whatever, girl." Julia rolled her eyes.

The next night, at precisely eight o'clock, Karen heard a knock on her door. She had spent an hour getting ready and felt silly, like a high school girl going to prom. The majority of that time had been spent selecting her outfit. He had told her to wear her white dress, but she had debated for a long while as to whether to follow his instructions. She already felt she was giving him too much power.

But, at the same time, another thought was swirling around her mind, one she was surprised to have. She couldn't quite make sense of it. It was a feeling of happiness and relief of not having to think of what to wear. It was also a feeling of satisfaction of knowing he would be pleased to see her wearing his favorite dress and her sexy red Louboutin pumps. Looking herself over in her full length mirror, she told herself she still had time to change. *No, hell with it. I'm wearing this because I like it. He just happens to like it, too.*

But when she opened the door and saw his quick smile as his eyes looked her over, her heart skipped a beat. She was surprised to realize she thoroughly enjoyed his pleased expression. *Well, I'll be damned.*

"Are you ready, beautiful?"

"Yes, I am. Where are we going?"

He made a tsk-tsk sound. "I can't tell you. It's a surprise."

He took her hand and led her to his car. "Nice ride," she commented.

"Thank you. I bought it when I graduated a few months back. A little congratulations to me gift."

"Well, I like it. Nice choice."

It was a blue BMW 5 series. She wondered

how the hell he afforded that right after law school but decided not to ask. For all she knew, his dad bought it for him. She always thought he looked like a spoiled rich boy; now it all made sense.

He walked around to the passenger side and opened her door, waiting while she stepped inside. Seeing her facial expression, he said, "Chivalry is not dead, Miss Sanders."

"I see that."

When they arrived at Amberley's, Brad guided her through the restaurant following the hostess to their table. His hand rested gently on the small of her back as they walked.

He pulled out her chair and she sat, looking around the restaurant. Mostly couples filled the room, but there was a large family sitting in the center of the room at a long table. Wineglasses clinked, echoing around the room like tiny bells. The sound of laughter from happy couples filled the air and a soft symphony trickled from the speakers nestled inconspicuously in the shadows above the windows. Karen's eyes rested on four antique paintings lined up along the wall adjacent to their table. Housed in ornate bronze frames, two of the paintings were black and white and two were in sepia tones. They were of the same little girl but she was doing something different in each picture. One in particular caught Karen's eye. The girl was sitting cross-legged in the grass, studying a daisy she held between her fingers. She looked so peaceful and serene. It made Karen wonder if she had ever been that relaxed.

"Penny for your thoughts?"

"I was just taking it all in. This place is beautiful."

Brad followed her gaze. "It is." He looked back at her. "Not as beautiful as you."

Karen laughed. "Well played, sir, well played."

He shrugged. "Well, it's true."

"You're trying to romance me, aren't you?"

"Is it working?"

Karen narrowed her eyes.

"I do like you, Karen. And something tells me you've never been properly romanced before."

"Oh really? And what makes you think that?"

"You seem...well, you were complaining about men the other day and you seem frustrated."

"That obvious, huh? Well, I haven't had any luck in that department. Like I said, men are threatened by a successful woman. I guess I'm not domesticated enough."

"And I told you that not all men are like that."

"I *can* cook though."

"Well, that's good to know." He paused, running a hand through his dark hair. "Do you really believe that, though? I mean, don't you think it's a fallacy to generalize all men based on your experiences?"

Karen laughed. "You sound like a lawyer. Of course, that can't be true. But, I have yet to meet someone who isn't like that, so..." She trailed off. "Then tell me. You keep saying not all men are like that, so you must be talking about yourself. Why are you so different? Or are you just saying that to get into my pants?"

Brad smirked. "I think that ship has sailed."

Karen threw a crouton across the table at him, which he dodged just in time. It landed on the floor next to an elderly couple in the corner who were sipping from tiny espresso cups. She looked at them apologetically and shrugged, pointing to Brad. The woman smiled.

"I am different, Karen. If you paid attention, you'd see that."

"Oh, I pay attention. Tell me how an Ivy League golden boy ends up being Mr. Chivalrous and not threatened by successful women. Especially considering your age. I mean, no offense, but you're young and...well, you can't possibly be that mature."

Brad pushed his plate aside and leaned forward, resting his forearms on the table, and folded his hands. "Okay. First of all, you know this, but I'll remind you again. I'm only a few years younger than you. And second of all, I grew up fast. I had to."

"Why?"

"I'm the oldest of four kids. I have two sisters and a brother. When I was twelve, my dad left and we never saw him again. I still don't know why he left. They were fighting a lot, but I never saw him since and my mom refused to talk about it. Anyway, she was devastated but she kept going, working three jobs at one point. She worked her ass off to take care of us, but I could see how hard it was for her. I did as much as I could around the house, cooking dinner every night, doing the laundry, helping my brother and sisters with their homework. Over the next few years, she kept getting thinner and thinner and she was just so tired all the time. I thought it was just stress. She told me not to worry, that she was just tired. But, I knew something was wrong. I just didn't know how bad it was. A month after I turned sixteen, she was put into the hospital. She had pancreatic cancer. I wasn't supposed to hear this, but I was listening to the doctors talk outside the room, and I overheard one of them say she had three months to live if she was lucky." He paused to take a deep breath and bit his lip. "She lived another four months after that. Our uncle moved in for a while, became our legal guardian, but he had an alcohol problem. We ended up getting into a nasty fight. He attacked me and I punched him, gave him a black eye. He left and never came back. So I took care of them for the next several years."

"By yourself?"

Brad nodded and picked up his glass of wine. "By myself." He sipped then set it down and looked away. His eyes were distant, as if he were looking at a movie of his life on a screen across the room, remembering the events.

Karen sighed. "Wow. Brad." She reached across the table and took his hand. "I had no idea. That's intense. I'm so sorry." After a moment, she said, "Yet you ended up becoming a lawyer. Quite impressive."

He nodded. "I always got good grades in school and wanted to go into law since I was nine." He laughed, shaking his head. "I don't know why. I just knew."

"You like to fight for people."

He squeezed her hand. "I do. Yeah, that must be it."

"So, how did you end up going to Harvard?"

"Baseball scholarship. Full ride. I still worked a part time job the whole time, saved money. That's how I got the car," he said, motioning with his head to the parking lot. "I wanted to be comfortable and never have to live like my mom did. I think the heartbreak and stress killed her. I think that kind of stuff can give you cancer."

"I think so, too," Karen said quietly.

He suddenly sat up taller in his chair and sighed loudly as if to shake off the emotion of the conversation. "I haven't told anyone that in a long time."

"I'm glad you told me." She stared into his dark eyes, noticing the ever-present cockiness was missing and in its place was a naked vulnerability.

SEVEN

Her house was a two-story Victorian nestled in the town of Brookline on the outskirts of the city. Dark red with blue-grey trim and subdued yellow shutters, it was her castle. She had bought it a year ago for dirt-cheap and had it remodeled. All her stress melted away when she stepped inside at the end of each day. Her friends told her she was crazy for buying such a big house on her own, but she knew it was a good investment. She wanted to have a family one day.

"I meant to tell you earlier. I love your place. It looks like a gothic dollhouse," Brad said as they pulled into her driveway.

"Gothic?" Karen looked over at him as he turned off the engine.

"It suits you."

She laughed. "I've never thought of it as gothic, but I love it. It has character."

Brad took her hand as he walked her to her front door. She surprised herself by not pulling away. His hand felt so warm, so strong. It was comforting. Her mind was still reeling from all the new information about him. He had had a rough life. And to think she assumed he was some spoiled rich boy that went to Harvard.

Before she could change her mind, she asked, "Would you like to come in?"

He smiled and pulled her closer, wrapping his arms around her shoulders.

"Are you sure? Once we cross this line, we can never go back."

She rolled her eyes. "Come on," she said, pulling his hand as she led him inside.

"Would you like a drink?" She asked as she led him to the kitchen.

He looked skeptical. "Are you trying to get me drunk so you can take advantage of me?"

"I think that ship has sailed, don't you?"

"Touché." He smiled. "Sure, I'd love one."

"Scotch ok?" She bent down to the bottom cupboard and pulled out a bottle of Macallan.

He raised his eyebrows. "Scotch would be great. I didn't take you for a scotch girl."

"No? Well, my dad always drank it and I used to hate it. But, I started raiding the liquor cabinet in high school and it grew on me." She walked over to the cupboard where she kept her glasses. Her hip grazed his pants as she brushed by him. It was a tight squeeze, but he didn't move to give her room.

"Did you get into trouble when you were younger?"

"No, I was good at covering my tracks. I used

to sneak out and spend the night with my boyfriend. I'd sneak back in before everyone got up in the morning. They never knew." She filled two glasses and then felt him swat her behind.

"Bad girl!"

Karen laughed as she handed him his glass. "You sound surprised."

"I guess I shouldn't be. I thought you were really uptight when I first met you. I was honestly surprised when you let me kiss you in your office. I thought for sure you were going to slap me." He laughed.

"I almost did."

"Why didn't you?"

"I wanted to kiss you. I was tired of trying to deny it."

"You don't always have to be in control."

"I feel like I do. But, sometimes I just want to let go. It gets exhausting. And you're pretty irresistible, you know that?"

"Am I now?"

"You are. Let's go sit down."

He followed her to the living room but as soon as she set down her glass, he pushed her onto the couch and laughed at her expression.

"You don't waste any time, do you?"

"I don't like to waste time with you. I find you incredibly irresistible too. I like helping you surrender control."

"That's so nice of you." She laughed. "You're good at it."

"I know."

"Cocky much?"

"A lot."

"I know. Now come here." She pulled him down on top of her.

He kissed her but stopped and inched back towards her feet and slipped off her shoes. Working his way up her leg, he planted soft kisses along her skin. Her legs trembled and she thought it felt different this time. He was being gentler. There were no power games, no dirty talk. He took his time and she savored every sensation. When he entered her, he started slow and rhythmic, unlike his usual hard thrusting. She felt vulnerable looking up at him; he was staring intently into her eyes.

"How does that feel, sweetheart?"

She moaned. "You feel amazing."

"Good," he said as he kept up the slow rhythm, leaning down to kiss her neck and collarbone.

She grabbed a handful of his hair and said into his ear, "Give it to me hard."

She heard his low, soft laugh. "As you wish, Miss Sanders." He pulled back and slammed into her, making her cry out. "Is that better?"

"God, yes."

A few hours later, thoroughly spent from their long sex session, she rolled over to glance at the clock. It was 2:00 AM. She thought about how different it had been tonight. There had been none of Brad's playful punishment, no spanking, no roughness. It had been sweet and sensual. She glanced over at Brad, his face slowly coming into focus in the dim light from the moon through the window. He was fast asleep. He looked so boyish, so peaceful and serene, his eyelids twitching every few seconds. *I wonder what he's dreaming about.* Then she shook her head and laughed to herself. *I'm watching him sleep. This is like a bad Lifetime movie.* She inched closer to him and rested her head on the pillow again. He made a sleepy sound and wrapped his arm around her, pulling her in tight.

On the following Monday, Karen found Brad in the hallway. He had his briefcase strapped onto his shoulder and was looking down at his phone.

"It's about eleven thirty. Are you ready?"

"Born that way."

"Okay, hot shot. Just follow my lead. When it doubt, keep it shut," she said, pointing to his lips.

"There's no need to treat me like a child, Karen. I know how to behave."

"Yeah, well, you're a baby lawyer and you have a lot to learn," she said.

Brad laughed. "A *baby* lawyer? That had better mean that I represent toddlers, because—"

"Yeah, yeah. Believe what you want. But, trust me. Let me take the lead on this." She leaned in and whispered in his ear. "And you can take the lead later tonight."

He shook his head but smiled. "I see how it is."

She sighed loudly. "Well, good! I was wondering when you'd finally get it!"

"Okay, smart-ass. They're waiting."

They rode together to the Hilton Garden Inn where the client had requested the meeting take place.

"God, it's hot. Why did I wear pants?" Karen tugged at her black dress pants. She could feel beads of sweat trickling down her legs.

"I have no idea. You look better without them," Brad said.

Karen gave him a playful punch in the arm. "I wish I'd worn a skirt or a dress."

"Yeah, but I'm glad you didn't, because it would be too tempting for me to reach my hand under the table and feel you up during lunch."

They strode into the hotel and made their way to the restaurant where they saw Mrs. Michelle Hendricks sitting alone at a table covered in a white cloth. She was staring at the candle in the center of the table, her hand holding a large wine glass filled with water. She tapped her nails against the glass, making a *tink-tink-tink* sound. She bit her lip and looked up when she saw Karen and Brad approaching.

She stood. "Ms. Sanders? Mr. Thomas?"

As they made their introductions, Karen suppressed a smile when she noticed Michelle staring at Brad. He seemed oblivious of his effect on her. After salads had been ordered and water glasses filled, Karen said, "Okay, Michelle. We've reviewed the information you faxed to us and we'd like to discuss how we can help you." She opened her briefcase and pulled out a black folder, laying it on the table. "Now, just to make sure I understand, you and your husband you are currently separated."

"That's right. He was cheating on me. I caught him with a co-worker."

"And he has also taken your daughter to live with him?"

"Yes, they are living at his new girlfriend's house. I don't like it; I don't even know her."

"What's your daughter's name?" Brad asked.

"Kate. She's seven." Michelle smiled at Brad.

"That's a beautiful name."

"Do you believe that Kate is in any danger?" Karen asked.

"I don't know. That's the worst part. I mean, Bill does drink, but I don't know if he does it around her. And like I said, I don't know his girlfriend."

"Okay, well we would be happy to help you. Do you think he would agree to mediation so you can keep this out of court?"

"Maybe. He's such an asshole. He hasn't let me see her in two weeks. Sorry for the language." She looked down at her salad and pushed around the lettuce with her fork.

Brad held up his hand. "No need to apologize. We understand. This is a very frustrating time for you. Let us help."

"Do you think I could get full custody?"

"I don't see why not. But, we can—"

Karen stopped him. "We don't want to make any promises. These cases can be complicated and if it goes to court, you never know what the judge will decide. But, we can get the ball rolling. If you choose to let us represent you, we will need some additional paperwork—"

"Most of the time, judges do side with the mother, so I wouldn't worry if I were you." Brad interjected.

Karen primly wiped her mouth with her linen napkin. "Will you excuse me? I need to run to the ladies room."

Michelle smiled and nodded. "Sure."

Walking fast to the other side of the restaurant, Karen was fuming. *I told him to keep his mouth shut! He's getting her hopes up.* She stepped into the ladies' room and pulled out her lipstick.

EIGHT

The bathroom door opened behind her. She knew it was him without even looking. Whirling around, she started towards him.

"Who the hell do you think you are?"

He looked confused. "I'm the guy who just landed the firm a new client."

"What?"

"When you walked away, she said she would definitely like to hire us."

"Yeah, because you're giving her false hope, telling her what she wants to hear. And you're in the ladies room. Get out."

They noticed the attendant standing quietly in the corner holding a stack of paper towels. The woman –whose nametag read Rose— looked at Brad. "Sir—"

But, Brad handed her a large bill and said,

"Five minutes."

Rose shrugged and walked out.

Karen rolled her eyes and turned away, mumbling under her breath, "Nice."

"Apparently we need to talk."

"No, we need to get back out there. She is going to wonder where we are."

Brad shook his head and looked at her patiently. "She's fine."

"God, you're naive."

Brad's eyebrows shot up. "Excuse me?"

"You don't know what you're doing yet. You have some nerve acting like you're some hotshot attorney who's been in the game for years. You should have let me handle it."

He sighed. "I don't see what the problem is. She hired us. End of story. Will you calm down?"

"I'll calm down when I think you understand how important it is to not get her hopes up right away, before we know enough about her case."

"You really need to have some faith in me. I wouldn't have said that if I didn't believe it."

She sighed loudly and ran her hands through her hair then walked over to the other side of the room.

Brad walked slowly over to her. She was looking in the mirror, fixing her hair. He came up behind her and whispered in her ear. "You're just mad because she likes me. You can't stand that I'm good at what I do and you weren't the star this time."

She tried to push him away. "You asshole. I'm glad you're good at what you do. Do you think you'd still be here if you weren't? And I don't always need to be the star. My point is that you took a huge risk in there. Now if we don't get her what she wants, she'll be devastated. So, no pressure for us. You can't do that again."

He pushed her hair to the side, exposing her neck. His eyes met hers in the mirror and he smiled. She stared back seriously. "I'm not kidding Brad. Do you understand?"

He smirked. "Yes, ma'am." He kissed her neck, making her shoulder rise involuntarily and sending a chill down her spine.

"Brad..." She felt her body begin to warm and she tried to pull away.

"No, none of that." He pulled one strap of her dress down over her shoulder.

"We can't, not here."

"Sure we can," he said, pulling the other strap down. He unhooked her bra and tossed it aside. Her breasts were exposed to the cold air and her nipples hardened. "So beautiful." He ran his palms lightly over her nipples and then slid his hands down, pushing her dress to the floor. She was wearing delicate lace panties in aquamarine.

"Ooh, I like these." He reached down and pulled them off. "But they have to go. We're going to get caught soon so we have to hurry a little. I promise I'll make it up to you later."

He unzipped his pants and pressed himself into her from behind. She couldn't wait to feel him inside her so she bent over the sink, giving him easier access.

"I know you will. Take me now," she said.

"Yes, Boss," he said, grabbing her hips, pulling her back to him.

He pushed himself inside her and reached

around to pleasure her.

"Mmm...Brad..." she moaned.

Her back arched, she met his eyes in the mirror. "Give it to me hard, Brad."

He held onto her hips, thrusting into her quickly. She reached down and touched herself until she felt the pressure build. "Getting close..." she breathed.

"Give it up, Karen. Now."

At the sound of his low commanding words, she exploded and rested her arms on the counter. "You're amazing..."

Brad pulled her up and kissed her. "*We're* amazing."

"And we'd better get out of here."

"We should, but don't you think it would be kind of hot if someone caught us?"

She laughed. "Maybe. But not if it was our client."

"You still mad at me?"

Sighing, she began putting her clothes back on and fixing her hair. "Maybe."

He smiled. "I can work with that."

"You can't just give me an orgasm every time I'm mad at you," she said.

He cocked his head to the side. "Why not? It seems to work."

She straightened his tie and gave him a peck on the cheek. "Let's get back out there."

NINE

The next day Ethan, Karen and Brad were in Karen's office for an impromptu meeting. As they were wrapping up, Karen sat behind her desk watching Ethan and Brad talk. *Brad looks especially hot today. Maybe a little lunchtime fun would be good.*

Karen was brought back to the present when Ethan said, "Good job on the Hendricks case. I heard you made her some promises, though. Make sure you follow through for her, all right?"

"Of course. I plan on it," Brad said, nodding.

Ethan patted him on the back and walked out of the room. Brad waited a beat then closed the door behind him and strode over to Karen, taking her face in his hands, kissing her. Just as he pulled away, the door opened behind them.

Karen heard an audible gasp.

"Oh. I can come back." It was Julia. *Thank*

God.

"No, come on in. I was just leaving." Brad's face darkened a shade as he nodded to Julia.

After the door had closed, Julia sat down in the chair across from where Karen was standing. She looked like the cat who swallowed the canary.

"Oh, just say it already," Karen crossed her arms.

"I don't know exactly what to say. I thought you weren't interested in him." She was smirking.

"Well, I guess I am." Karen sighed and walked over to her window. "I let this get out of hand."

"I won't tell anyone. Your secret is safe with me."

"I know, but what if that had been someone else?"

Julia said nothing.

"Exactly. I'm going to have to draw some boundaries. We can't get careless at work."

"It's really not a good idea. But from woman to woman: Go girl!"

Karen laughed. "Yeah, yeah. I need to do some damage control though. I know other people will start to catch on. When Ethan was just in here, he kept looking at me strangely. I think he knows. People can smell that sort of thing."

"What? All the dirty sex you're having?"

Karen shook her head but laughed. "Basically, yeah."

Julia's eyes widened. "Wait. Are you two doing it here after everyone else has left?"

"Of course not!"

"Right."

"That wasn't convincing, was it?"

Julia laughed. "Not at all." She stood to leave. "I'd better get back to work so I can leave on time and you guys can have your fun later."

"Oh, stop it. We aren't doing that anymore."

"Mmm-hmm," she said as she breezed out the door.

Karen spent the rest of the afternoon getting ahead on her work so she could relax that evening with Brad. They had been spending almost every night together, most of the time at her house. It was such a nice change to share her bed with someone, not to sleep alone. And she was starting to develop feelings for him. She just wasn't sure if he felt the same. She had let down her guard with him, which is something she had not done in a long time. Now she feared her vulnerability would open her up to be hurt by him. But, first she had to handle this work situation. There could be no more kissing at work, no more closed doors. Julia had already caught them and other people were starting to give her odd looks around the office.

When Brad walked down the hall a few minutes later, Karen called out, "Brad?"

He turned on his heel and walked in. Giving her a devilish grin, he started to close the door, but she stopped him. "No, leave the door open."

He looked mildly disappointed. "What's up?" He sat across from her.

She leaned in closer and said, "No more closed doors. No more...you-know-what. Ok?"

He gave a quick laugh. "You're being really paranoid."

Pushing her chair back violently, she stood. "Brad—"

Motioning for her to sit back down, he said, "Whoa, whoa. Okay, calm down. I understand. I just don't think anyone has any idea. And we can keep it that way."

She walked around the desk so she was standing directly in front of him. "I don't think you realize how hard I've had to work to get where I am. Julia already knows we're seeing each other, but that's fine. But if Ethan or anyone else finds out, I instantly lose credibility. They won't take me as seriously if they know I'm fucking the new attorney."

Brad stood and when she tried to back away, he grabbed her arms and held her in place. "Don't move," he said before striding over to the door and slamming it shut.

When he returned to her, he used his body to press her into the wall and kissed her roughly. "Brad, stop!" she said, wrenching out of his grasp.

Over Brad's shoulder, she caught a glimpse of movement and her heart sped up to a gallop when she saw Ethan standing in the doorway. "Is everything—" he started but then his eyes widened. "Karen? Everything okay here?"

"Yes, just fine." She took a deep breath and went to her desk, pretending to organize paperwork.

"I heard the door slam and I came to see—" He paused and looked at Brad, frowning. "Brad?"

"I was just leaving," Brad said as he strode quickly out of the room. Karen caught his angry – no, make that furious – facial expression in the mirror by the door as he walked out.

Ethan stood, dumbfounded. "What was that? Are you okay, Karen? Because that looked like—"

"No, it's fine. It was nothing."

"You would tell me if...I mean, he doesn't seem the type, but from what I just saw...you say the word, Karen. Because if that kid is harassing you, I'll—"

"No, no. Please, Ethan. Really. It was just a misunderstanding. Everything is fine, I assure you."

Ethan hesitated. "Okay. Well, you know you can talk to me about it. We don't tolerate any harassment at this office. Don't cover for him."

"I'm not. I promise."

"Well, all right then." Ethan sighed, ruffled his hair and made his way towards the door. He paused for a beat as if he was going to say something else, but then reconsidered and Karen watched him walk down the hall to his office.

Karen didn't see Brad the rest of the day and chalked it up to him sulking about being caught. She pulled out her phone from her top drawer and scrolled to Brad's name. She typed a message: That was exactly what I was talking about. I wasn't being paranoid. She clicked Send.

An hour later, she noticed he hadn't responded, so she decided to see if he was in his office. He wasn't. *Probably ducked out early, too embarrassed to face the rest of the day.* Walking back to her office, she decided to let him pout for a while. They could talk about it later that night.

But, he never called, never texted back. At eight o'clock, she called his cell and it went straight to voice mail. *Why the hell is he punishing me? He was in the wrong.* But as much as she tried to push aside her feelings and blame him, she felt lonely and empty. He would normally be sitting across the table from her right now, eating dinner, laughing. Suddenly, her house felt emptier than ever before. She lay in bed, staring at the ceiling, when a knock at the door startled her. *Good, he's here.*

TEN

When she opened the door, she noticed his face looked different somehow. The affectionate, loving gaze in his eyes was gone. His mouth was set to a thin line and his brows were furrowed.

"Brad! I was worried. I—" She reached out to hug him, but he pushed her away.

"We need to talk. Can I come in?"

"Of course." She opened the door wide and he walked straight to the couch and sat. "Look, I know you must be upset about earlier, but this is why—"

"Yeah, you told me so. Got it."

"No, that's not what I meant."

"Yeah, well," he said, pushing back his hair as he sighed. "It's exactly what you mean. You're not thinking of me. You're just thinking of you. You said yourself I was a baby lawyer. You don't take me seriously, you don't think my career is as important as yours. Do you know how that looked today? I know Ethan thought I was forcing myself on you. And you didn't even correct him."

"No, I told him—"

"What? Did you tell him we have been having a consensual relationship for weeks?"

"No, but—"

"That's what I thought. You couldn't possibly tell him the truth because it would make you look bad. So, just leave Brad out to dry, let them think the new guy is sexually assaulting you. You're unbelievable." He shook his head. "I thought you were a bitch when I first met you, but after getting to know you, I thought you were a great person. I thought I knew the real you. I guess I was right the first time." He stood from the table.

Karen stood up in front of him. "Wait. That's not fair, Brad. What was I supposed to say? I didn't know what to do. It caught me by surprise. Don't go. Let's talk, let's figure this out."

"I think it's already figured out. It's over, Karen. I'm done. I'm done being your piece of ass you can use whenever you want."

She exploded. "Are you kidding me? You seduced *me*! I think it's the other way around. You're just mad because you were thinking with the wrong head, insisting on kissing me in the office when I kept warning you that we were going to get caught!"

He took a step forward so they were nose to nose. "And you were right. We did get caught. Feel better now? And I took the fall for it, looking like some sex-crazed perv, forcing myself on my female colleague, while you look like the victim. So, congratulations. You win." He took her by the shoulders and gently moved her to the side so he could pass. "I hope it was fun for you." The heavy mahogany door slammed behind him, echoing throughout the house.

"I love you," she whispered to the door. In response, the orchid on the entryway table fell to the floor.

***

The next few days were pure misery. Brad was gone. The morning after their break-up, Karen had noticed his office was empty so she had marched to Ethan's office.

He was just hanging up the phone. "Oh, good. Karen, I need to talk to you."

"Did you fire him?" she spit out.

Ethan's eyebrows shot up. "Brad? No, he quit. He came in this morning and collected his things. He told me he could no longer work here and that was it. He walked out the door." He paused. "Aren't you glad? His behavior was inappropriate. I'm sorry you had to deal with that."

Karen sighed and sat down in the leather chair in front of Ethan's desk. "That's the thing, Ethan. Brad did nothing wrong."

Ethan frowned. "Well—"

"No, he shouldn't have kissed me in the office. But, it wasn't the first time. And it was consensual."

"I don't understand. You mean..." he trailed off.

Karen nodded. "Yes. We had been seeing

each other for a while."

Ethan leaned back in his chair and took a moment to respond. "What is a while?"

"A few weeks."

He nodded and looked out the window. After a couple of minutes, he said, "Well, you're both adults and can do what you want – outside of the office. But," he said, shaking his head. "Oh, Karen. These things get messy if you bring it to work."

"I know. I never meant to let it get out of control."

"I'm sure you didn't. I know this is quite out of character for you, too. You had a moment of weakness. Let's just get back on track, shall we?"

"Sounds good."

But, Karen couldn't focus the rest of the week. She wasn't sleeping and had no appetite. There was a cavernous hole inside her that was as painful as it was deep. On Friday night, she wrestled with the decision to call him. *He probably won't pick up anyway.* And she was right; when she dialed his number, it rang twice then went to voice mail. *He rejected my call. Well, that's encouraging.* After the beep, she said, "Brad, it's me. Look, I'm sorry. I was wrong. You were right; I was being selfish. I told Ethan the truth. I told him we had been seeing each other for weeks now. I know I should have told him that at the time. I made a huge mistake, Brad and I'm sorry. Please forgive me."

There was no response. Karen lay in bed all day Saturday, alternating between crying and sleeping. She woke up and judging by the dim orange light coming into her window, she guessed it was early evening. The clock read 6:01. Throwing the covers off of her, she took a deep breath. She jumped out of bed and took a shower. Hastily getting dressed, she threw on jeans, an old grey t-shirt and her army green Converse. She ran a comb through her hair and bolted out the door before she could change her mind.

As she was driving, the sky grew darker and thunder rumbled in the distance. By the time she got to his house, the rain was pouring down. His car was in the driveway and the house looked quiet. She carefully walked up the slippery concrete steps to his front door and rang the bell. When he didn't answer right away, she thought of turning around and running back to her car. She must have looked a mess, her hair soaked, her clothes dripping, but she decided to give it a couple more minutes. She knew she'd regret it if she didn't at least try. But after ringing the bell once more and no answer, she thought: *This is ridiculous. Go home.* But, just as she was turning to leave, she heard the *whoosh* of the door as it opened behind her. She slipped, lost her balance and fell, landing on her backside on the hard, wet concrete. She felt strong hands pulling her up by her arms and looked up to see his face, which wore an expression of worry with just a tinge of amusement.

He guided her inside, into the warm, dry foyer and closed the door behind her.

He was wearing jeans and a white cotton t-shirt. His inky hair was wet and dripping onto the tops of his shoulders. His dark eyes searched hers before looking her up and down. "Well, you sure made an entrance," he said, smirking. "Let me get you a towel." As he walked away, he turned his head slightly back to her. "I was in the shower. I hope you weren't standing out there too long."

When he came back with a blue bath towel, his eyes showed a mix of surprise and something else she couldn't quite put her finger on. She decided it was anger. Yeah, he was definitely still mad.

She decided to just come out with it. "Brad. I'm sorry. I know you're angry with me and I don't blame you."

He nodded. "I am."

"What I did was fucked up. I know that. I just...okay, I was being selfish. I wasn't thinking about you and I'm so sorry. I know I can't expect you to forgive me, but God, I just, oh Brad...I love you. I love you, okay? And these past few days have been torture for me. I—"

"Don't you own a raincoat or an umbrella?"

She frowned. "It wasn't raining when I left. I was a little too distracted to check the weather."

He pulled her close and took her face in his hands. "I love you, too."

Her heart leapt in her chest. She smiled and wrapped her arms around him, burying her face in his shoulder, taking in his soapy, masculine scent.

"I'm just going to have to teach you a lesson now. Go up to the bedroom and take off your clothes."

"All of them? But I'm so cold," she whined.

He stalked towards her. "Seriously?" He ran his hands up along the sides of her waist up to her breasts and stopped, circling his thumbs over her nipples. "Don't worry. I'll warm you up. Now go." He slapped her behind.

She rose up on her toes and kissed his cheek then turned and hurried up the stairs to his bedroom.

ABOUT THE AUTHOR

Adriana Blair grew up in a suburb just outside of Boston, Massachusetts as the only child of non-emotional parents who sent her to Saint Mary's Preparatory School for girls. She loved the skirts but found the doctrine hard to take. Fifteen minutes after graduating, she ripped off her nylons and hopped on a bus to Florida where she began to discover the joys and carnal pleasures of life.

Having lived in Florida for eighteen years, Adriana writes full time and volunteers at her local animal shelter. Besides writing, her favorite thing is music, and she listens to everything from Rammstein to Katy Perry. If you liked *Punishable by Law*, stay tuned for more naughty tales and stories of romance from Adriana on Amazon.com/AdrianaBlair.Author.

Adriana loves to hear from readers so feel free to drop her a line at adrianablair@outlook.com.

www.ingramcontent.com/pod-product-compliance
Lightning Source LLC
Chambersburg PA
CBHW020639130626
46552CB00003B/1302